Tillsonbugger Adventures

The Swarm that Swarmed

A Short Story

Written by Fernanda Lazzaro

Illustrated by Qi Zhan

Tillsonbugger Adventures, a series of children's books geared primarily for seven to ten year-old readers, originated with author Fernanda Lazzaro's experience as a backyard beekeeper. The first book in the series, "The Swarm that Swarmed", is based on an incident when Fernanda's neighbour became frightened as her bees swarmed their tree. Fernanda's distress at her neighbour's reaction — burning down the branch that held the bees, prompted her to write a children's book to communicate the importance of bees.

It's even an enjoyable story for adults (like me!). I definitely recommend it to anyone who wants a sweet story about young friends and their summer adventure.

- Ginger Mom and the Kindle Quest

This will be a great addition to our school library! The illustrations will appeal to kids and the author does a good job combining a storyline with facts. Bugs are a very popular subject with students.

- Elementary School Librarian

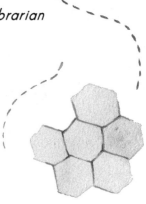

WELCOME TO TILLSONBUG

All are welcome in Tillsonbug!

It has plenty of flowers and leafy trees,

For the bugs to bug and the bees to bee.

You can walk or run in the morning sun,

Or lay in the grass 'til the day is done.

Mother Nature will give you a hug,

No matter who you are in Tillsonbug.

Written by Mike Galic

The narrow Alton River runs for miles and miles across the county of Cadee, weaving in and out of green rolling hills. Hidden in the valley, where the east meets west, lies the town of Tillsonbug, so tiny that it could be missed in the blink of an eye.

On the left side of Main Street, one will find a convenience store that sells worms and ice cream (not

'worm ice cream' but worms and ice cream separately, found at opposite ends of the shop). Next to the convenience store is the library that is much larger on the inside than it looks on the outside, and a hardware store.

On the right sit the farmer's market, the post office, and the elementary school.

Tia, Vivian, and Fil had lived in Tillsonbug all their lives. Fil (short for Filbert) and Vivian were brother and sister—twins in fact, but not identical twins. Tia and the twins were in grade four. Another summer break had arrived, and the twins planned to spend it like all the other kids—sleeping in and watching cartoons. Tia, however, believed that watching cartoons was for toddlers.

After she had had a healthy breakfast and tidied her room, Tia had set aside some time for grooming herself. She would not leave the house on any occasion without looking proper, and going out to play with her two best friends was no exception.

Tia was about to finish her ensemble with a hair bow, when she noticed a bee buzzing around in her room. Terrified, she ran out of

the house to the twins' house, only half a loop tied in her satin hair ribbon. Walking over to their house would usually be a ten-minute affair, but this time, she reached within sixty seconds!

Vivian and Fil were sitting by the creek in their backyard and munching on donuts, when their usually prim-and-proper friend ran to them, looking completely dishevelled.

"Did you see a ghost or something?" Vivian exclaimed. "Why on earth do you look like that?"

Trying to catch her breath so that she could explain her terror, Tia noticed the sugary treats Vivian and Fil were eating. "Donuts? First thing in the morning? Honestly! That's no way to feed a growing body!"

"It's not morning anymore. It's afternoon," Fil mumbled, his mouth full.

I'M NO INSECT! I'M PROUD TO BE AN ARACHNID.

Tia shook her head in disapproval, allowing the half-bow in her hair to unloop itself. She looked up and screamed, "Bees! They're haunting me!"

The twins looked up too and saw hundreds of bees overhead, flying towards a nearby tree on the property. Unable to contain their excitement, the two jumped up to follow the insects. But Tia kept her distance from the bees and the siblings, who were now standing right below the branch on which the busy, buzzing bees had gathered.

"Are you two crazy? Are you looking to get stung?" Tia whispered, terrified.

"It's not like they're creepy insects, like spiders or something!" Vivian emphasized. "Hey, you want—"

"There's no way I'm staying here, with those things in my vicinity! Honestly!" Tia interrupted her.

"Please don't go home, Tia! Fil and I will get rid of them!" Vivian pleaded.

"We will?" a confused Fil asked, turning to his sister.

"Let's go to the market and get some honey," Vivian continued, ignoring Fil. There was no point arguing with Vivian once she had made up her mind.

Fil and Tia plodded along reluctantly, listening to Vivian passionately declare her desire to save the bees. "They're becoming extinct, you know. Now is our chance to do something about that. Who knows what they're running from, the poor things!"

After a while, the trio returned to the backyard with two pails of honey.

"You two can direct the bees to that tree over there!" Tia suggested, pointing to a tree on the other side of the water and quickly taking a few steps back to avoid any contact with the insects.

"I'll sit on Fil's shoulders and wave a twig with honey on it, so they can smell it. After that, we can guide them to that tree!" Vivian asserted, extremely proud that she had thought of something so clever.

But, after about a minute of trying to lure the bees, the children did not have much success.

"Hey! You're dropping honey all over me!" Fil complained, shielding his face.

"Shush! I'm trying to concentrate!" responded Vivian.

The squabble between Fil and Vivian continued until Fil lost his balance, and they found themselves on the ground, covered in honey. The more they squirmed about, the more they seemed to get glued together.

In a desperate attempt to help her friends, Tia reached over to give Vivian and Fil a hand, curbing her fear of the hovering insects. But she too slipped and fell into the sticky mess.

"For the love of honeycombs! My dress!" Tia moaned.

Unable to contain their giggles any longer, the twins burst into laughter. Even Tia joined in, laughing at their sticky situation.

Fil had a sudden brainwave. "A honey trail! We'll make a trail to the tree!" he exclaimed.

"Shouldn't we clean ourselves first?" Tia asked.

"Nah. . . let's wash off after we've finished the trail. We're on a roll," Fil hollered, flashing a bright smile.

With the second pail in hand, Fil poured the honey straight onto the ground and walked backwards as the girls guided him towards the tree—walking backwards as well!

"More to the left. A little to your right," the girls instructed in unison.

"How will we get the honey to stick to the waterrrrrr. . ." Vivian wondered, while losing her footing at the edge of the creek. She grabbed onto Tia, who then grabbed onto Fil.

And that is how all three of them ended up splashing into the shallow water. The pail of honey flew up in the air and landed on Fil's head.

Fil, not even a bit amused, removed the pail from his head and said, "How will we get the honey to stick to the water? Oh, I don't know. Maybe we can make a bridge connecting the three of us and pour honey all over us. Oh! Wait! We already have honey all over us, Vivian!"

"Okay, enough you two! If anyone should be upset, it should be me! My dress smells like the creek! Eww!" Tia wailed.

Slowly, the children washed off the honey and sat by the creek, drying in the sun.

No bees could be seen on the honey trail. Neither were they in the air. There were no bees anywhere, except for the branch of the tree. . . near the house.

"I'm hungry," Fil spoke up. "Hey, let's get some ice cream!"

He led the two girls to the convenience store, where they picked their preferred flavours. Fil chose a concoction of chocolate chip, caramel, mint, and mango ice cream, making Vivian and Tia cringe in disgust as all of it was mushed into one large sugar cone. Vivian picked the pistachio ice cream in a regular cone, while Tia chose vanilla in a small cup.

"I don't trust what they put in these flavoured ice cream, and I highly doubt the cone is natural," Tia commented disdainfully.

Since the library was next door, Vivian got an idea. "Let's go and find some information about bees!" she suggested.

"You want ME to go in THERE on my summer break?" Fil responded, rolling his eyes. "What did they put in your pistachios? Nuts?"

Fil laughed at his own joke while Tia and Vivian made their way into the library. Fil soon followed after he finished his ice cream.

They found a book on bee pollination, and other "bee facts".

The queen bee is the leader of the honey bee colony.

The worker bees are all females.

Only female bees have stingers.

VIVIAN: "EVERYTHING IS ALWAYS BETTER WHEN A GIRL IS THE BOSS!"

TIA: "GIRL BEES ARE BETTER THAN BOY BEES."

FIL: "SEE, EVEN GIRL BEES ARE MEANER THAN BOY BEES!"

5.

This is the way some fruits, vegetables, and flowers grow and multiply.

1.

The female bee lands on a flower to drink the nectar, which she later turns into honey.

2.

If it is a "boy" flower, it will contain pollen. The pollen sticks to the bee's legs.

4.

That flower will then be fertilized by the pollen, which will make seeds.

3.

Some of the pollen will rub off her legs when she visits a "girl" flower of the same plant.

The children felt somewhat defeated after leaving the library. They still had not learned the reason all those bees were on the branch in their backyard. They sat down on the curb just outside the library.

"Those poor bees! They do so much for us. I wonder what scared them, eh?" Vivian asked.

"At least we tried to get them out of the tree. Maybe something was following them," Tia speculated.

At that moment, Farmer Drone was leaving the hardware store when he overheard the children. He walked over to them and said, "I was wondering why my beehive was partially full this morning. Those must be my bees in your tree."

"Farmer Drone? Why did the bees run away?" Vivian asked.

"They aren't running," the wise gentleman added with a chuckle, "They're swarming. You see, they outgrew the home I gave them,

so they're hanging out on your branch until they find a new home—somewhere cozy and safe. Next time you see this happen, you can call a beekeeper, like myself, and we can remove the bees without harming them. I'll take a look at them now. I was just on my way home. Be good now, kids."

"Thank you, Mr. Drone," the children chimed together.

"WOW! I feel like my brain has grown larger!" Tia exclaimed.

Fil did not want to admit it, but he did agree with her. After all, he had a reputation to maintain. "I think it should be illegal to learn anything when we're not in school. Umm, you girls want to go fishing? I'll grab some worms."

"Okay, as long as we keep the fish in the water," Vivian declared.

"And as long as I don't have to touch the worms!" Tia warned.

And so, on the first day of their summer break, in the tiny town of Tillsonbug, three young people learned that even the small things in life can make a big difference.

-THE END-